LET'S READ!

📖 Read the Page

▶ Read the Story

⭐ Game

⭐ Level 1   ⭐⭐ Level 2

↻ Repeat

⏹ Stop

INDL 3304.3

Disney · PIXAR

MONSTERS
UNIVERSITY

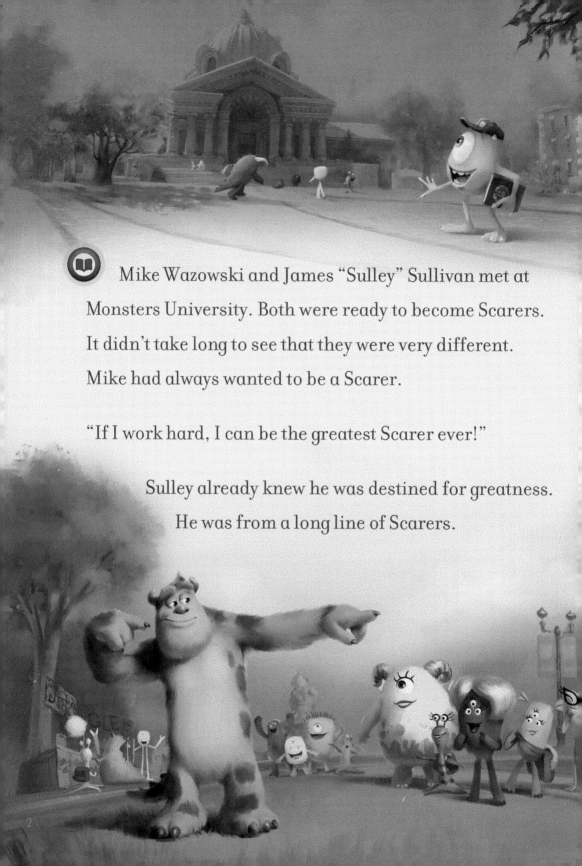

Mike Wazowski and James "Sulley" Sullivan met at Monsters University. Both were ready to become Scarers. It didn't take long to see that they were very different. Mike had always wanted to be a Scarer.

"If I work hard, I can be the greatest Scarer ever!"

Sulley already knew he was destined for greatness. He was from a long line of Scarers.

"Study all you want, little guy. A monster like you
will never be a Scarer." Sulley laughed.

3

On the day of the scare finals,
Mike and Sulley got into a scare-off.
When Mike unleashed his most frightening
roar, Sulley was not impressed.

"ROAR!" Sulley bellowed down at Mike.

Suddenly, Sulley knocked over
Dean Hardscrabble's prized
scream can.

It released an ear-piercing scream as it flew across the room! Hardscrabble was not happy.

After she gave Mike and Sulley their final exams, Hardscrabble kicked both of them out of the Scaring Program.

Being a Scarer was Mike's big dream and he was not going to give up.

"I've got it! All I have to do is win the Scare Games!" He'd prove that he deserved to be in the program.

Mike teamed up with a fraternity called Oozma Kappa, or OK. But they were still one monster short, so Sulley volunteered. Sulley was the last monster Mike wanted on his team.

Mike and Sulley had very different ideas about how to win the Scare Games. They couldn't work together as a team. The Oozma Kappas soon got discouraged.

Mike needed a new plan.

"We're going on a little field trip," he announced. That night, the OKs sneaked onto the roof of Monsters, Inc.

A scare floor was buzzing with activity. Mike asked his team to look at what the Scarers had in common. They all agreed that it was nothing. "The best Scarers use their differences to their advantage!" said Mike.

The OKs were inspired, and as the competition continued, the team began to work well together.

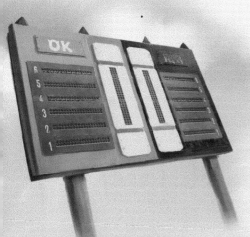

This new teamwork got Oozma Kappa into the final event of the Scare Games.

Meanwhile, Hardscrabble reminded Sulley that Mike was just not scary. Sulley told Hardscrabble she was wrong, but he was worried.

The final event took place in a scare simulator. Each competitor had to perform a scare. Mike was the last to go. He crept slowly and stealthily to the bed with the robot child and roared his scariest roar! The scream can filled immediately to the top! Oozma Kappa won the Scare Games!

Later, after everyone had left, Mike discovered that Sulley had rigged the simulator so Mike would get the highest score.

"You don't think I'm scary!"

Determined to prove himself, Mike broke into the Door Tech Lab and activated a door.

He crept through the door and into ...

... a cabin full of kids!

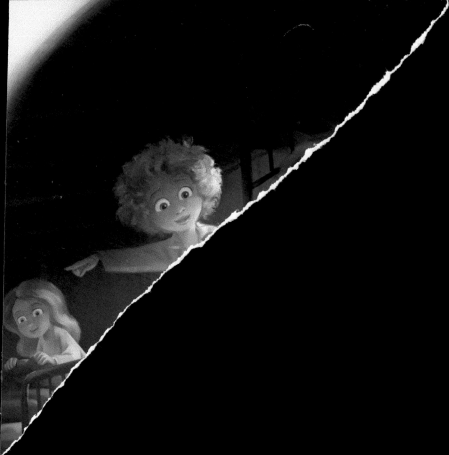

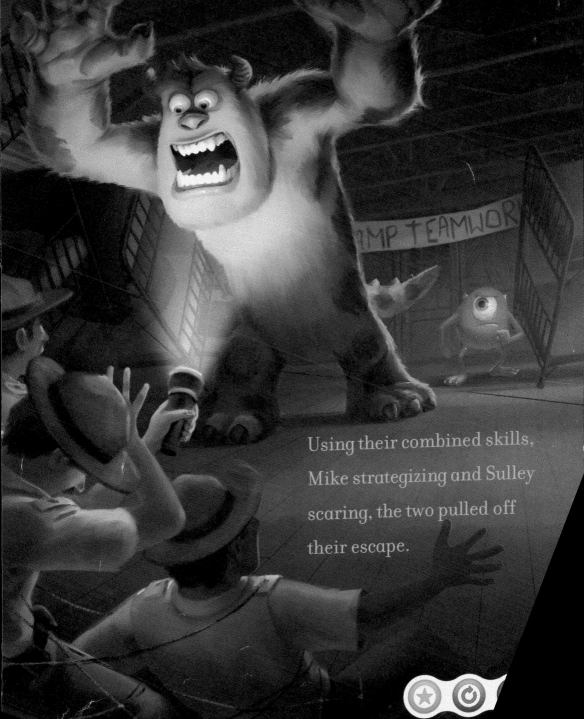

Using their combined skills, Mike strategizing and Sulley scaring, the two pulled off their escape.

Together, the monsters executed a monumental scare. They generated enough energy to not only power-up the door back to MU, but to fill every scream can in the Door Tech Lab!

Mike and Sulley had been expelled. They didn't know what they would do next.

"Mike, you're not scary, not even a little, but you are fearless!" said Sulley.

Dean Hardscrabble had been very surprised by the duo's final scare performance. She bid them farewell and wished them good luck. Then Mike noticed something in the school newspaper ... an ad for a job at Monsters, Inc.!

"We work at Monsters, Inc.!" exclaimed Mike.
Mike and Sulley got jobs in the mailroom.
They were the hardest workers Monsters, Inc.
had ever seen. Team Wazowski and Sullivan
were clearly destined for greatness!

Scare Class Classified

Noun

spider

snake

bear

lightning

the dark

tiger

Verb

creeping

roaring

hiding

growling

howling

leaping